The Chocolate Lab

By **ERIC LUPER**

Scholastic Inc.

For Elaine
(who has put up with my Cocoa-like
antics for many years)

ISBN 978-0-545-60166-5

12 11 10 9 8 7 6 5 4   15 16 17 18 19/0

Printed in the U.S.A.   40

First printing, September 2014
Designed by Sharismar Rodriguez

Chapter 1

Doggy Disaster

There are two kinds of people in this world, the kind who like dog licks and the kind who don't. I'm that first kind. I like the feel of sloppy, smooth dog tongue on my hand. I like warm dog breath in my face. I like knowing each drop of slippery slobber means my dog loves me no matter what. Most days my mom and dad are dog-lick people, too.

But not today. Today my parents want nothing to do with Cocoa's tongue or any of the rest of him. Today they just want a do-over so they can keep Cocoa out of the chocolate laboratory at the back of our chocolate shop and away from the display my mother was working on for next week's big Chocolate Expo.

"That dog . . ." my mom says as she looks at what's left of her workshop. "That . . . dog . . ."

Those are the only two words she says, but I can tell the rest of them are bunched up inside her mouth and want to burst right out.

I try to change the subject. "Did you ever think how amazing it is that we have a *chocolate* Labrador retriever with a *chocolate* name who lives in a *chocolate* shop who goes completely bonkers when he smells *chocolate*? It's like a miracle right here in our own house!"

And it's true. Cocoa may not be allowed to eat chocolate, but he can sniff it out from a mile away. When he does, he gets more excited than a cat with a noseful of catnip. I guess Cocoa is like me that way, because when I get an idea I can't sit still until I do something about it, too. Maybe that's why I know what he did is not actually his fault.

"I just wish our little miracle pooch would stay out of the workshop," Dad says. "How many times have we told you to put Cocoa in his crate when Mom is working?"

"I did," I say. "I remember locking it and everything."

"If you had locked Cocoa's crate, he wouldn't have been able to do this," Dad says. He dumps a tray of chocolates into the garbage. The smushed, smashed, totally mangled candies slide into the can with a *thumpity, thump, thump* louder than Fourth of July fireworks. Call me crazy, but I think they still look yummy.

"This isn't the first time, Mason," Mom says. "You're going into fifth grade. What have we told you about responsibility?"

ot sure if this is one of those don't-answer-it-or-you'll-be-in-big-fat-trouble questions, so I'm glad when my little sister, Hannah, walks in from our apartment upstairs. Her eyes roam over the mess. Pots and pans of every size litter the floor. Trays are upturned. Dark, gooey chocolate splatter covers everything like spin art gone wrong. Chocolate is even dripping from the ceiling!

Hannah narrows her eyes and looks around some more. "*Humph*" is all she says.

Mom puts her hand on Dad's arm. "Bill, even if I work twenty-four hours a day for the next week, there's no way we'll be ready for the expo. Not to mention the cost of what that dog . . . That . . . dog . . ."

Miss Meredith, Towne Chocolate Shoppe's only employee and definitely not a dog-lick person, begins straightening boxes next to the cash register. Cocoa waddles up next to me and noses at my hand. I know it's not the time for petting, but I give him a quick one anyway. He licks my fingertips.

"What if we all pitch in?" I say. I pick up a large spoon and straighten it as best I can. It's still bent.

"I couldn't do it with an army of Oompa Loompas," Mom says. "If Mel Kunkle could see us now, he'd be laughing his head off."

Mel Kunkle. Just the name gets my dad's face redder than a bowlful of cherry filling. Three years ago the Kunkles moved here from the big city with what Dad calls "big-city money." They also came with big-city ideas of how to put our small-town chocolate shop out of business. Not only did they put ads for Kunkle Kandies on every billboard, park bench, and diner place mat in town but they also bought a giant machine that burps out more chocolates in an hour than we can make in a week. People line up just to get a peek at the machine in their front window.

"No one is interested in quality anymore," Mom says, placing a drippy pan on the counter. "They want fancy gizmos and bright blinking lights. When Grandpa Irving gets here, we'll ask him to stay the week like we discussed."

"The week?!" Hannah and I say at once. Grandpa Irving is my dad's father, the side of the family that knows nothing about the magic of candy making. His idea of a fun weekend is dressing up in old army clothes, sleeping in a leaky tent, and pretending he doesn't know what electricity is. He never stops talking about the American Revolution, which is probably because he's old enough to owe George Washington a quarter.

Dad makes uggy-buggy eyes at Mom and she nods. It's how they talk to each other without words.

"We were going to take you guys for pizza to talk about this, but you might as well know now," Dad says. "We need to start thinking about the future. College for you two. Retirement someday. Even though we love Towne Chocolate Shoppe, we can't go on struggling. Your mother and I are going up to Glens Falls to see about a few things."

Mom drops a spatula and some dipping forks into the sink. "We may have to move in with Grandpa for a while, just until we sort things out."

"How long is a while?" Hannah asks. "School starts soon. I'm going to be head pirate in the fall musical. Mrs. Pratt said so when I saw her at the supermarket."

Dad unplugs the chocolate warmer. "One of

the reasons we need to go to Glens Falls is to look into school for you guys," he says.

"But what about the store?" I say.

Dad sighs. "Business has dropped off since Kunkle Kandies came to town. We were hoping the Chocolate Expo would help us get back on our feet."

"We can only keep this place open if it's making money," Mom adds.

"What about Cocoa?" I say. "Grandpa's building doesn't allow pets."

Mom slides the registration folder for the Chocolate Expo into the trash and cups my face in her hands. "Try not to worry, Mason. Your father and I will figure something out."

I look past Mom to the garbage can, and it looks like they've already figured out plenty. If that folder had a tongue, it would've been sticking it out at me.

Cocoa makes a chuffing sound as though he wants me to pull the folder out. Then I realize he's trying to tell me his superpowerful ears hear someone coming up the walk.

The door swings open and Miss Meredith stuffs her cell phone into her pocket. "Welcome to Towne Chocolate Shoppe," she says brightly. When she sees who it is, her smile vanishes and she pulls out her cell phone again.

Grandpa Irving is standing there with a suitcase tucked under one arm, a bundle of rolled-up maps under the other, and a tattered tricorn hat on his head. His eyebrows look bushier than ever.

"Where are my two favorite grandkids?" he bellows in his big-belly voice.

"We're your only grandkids!" Hannah says like she does every time he says that.

Grandpa looks around the store. "Sheesh,

did Virginia's Second Regiment march through here or something?"

Dad explains what happened while I go over and give Grandpa the strongest bear hug I can.

He fake groans from my squeeze and bends down (this time giving a real old guy achy-back groan). Maps spill from under his arm. "Don't you worry about this," he says. "Everything is going to be just fine."

But everything isn't going to be just fine. Towne Chocolate Shoppe, our family business, is going to close. Hannah and I will have to go to a new school, away from all our friends. And worst of all, Cocoa is going to live in some kennel somewhere with a bunch of dogs he doesn't even know.

I look for Hannah so we can figure out what to do, but she's already stomped away.

"Now, this is how a real man makes breakfast," Grandpa Irving says as he pokes at the campfire he's built in the middle of our backyard.

I look at the dented tin pot sitting on the crackling pile of embers. "What are you making?"

"It's called mush," Grandpa says proudly. "Mush mixed with a few secret ingredients of my own."

I lean forward and take a few tiny hamster sniffs. Whatever is bubbling in there smells spicy, sweet, and cinnamony all at the same time. I even catch a faint whiff of black licorice.

Hannah wrinkles her nose. "At last year's safety assembly, they told us open fires are illegal."

"Hogwash," Grandpa says. "Before stoves, people always cooked over fires."

"But we have a stove," I say.

"And breakfast cereal," Hannah adds. "I want a bowl of Frosted Fruit-Yums."

"You haven't lived until you've had my mush." Grandpa stirs the goop in the tin pot like he's some sort of top chef. The stink gets stronger and my eyes begin to water instead of my mouth. "It's the number one most popular dish at every reenactment I go to," he says.

"That's probably because everyone at these things eats grilled squirrel and turtle burgers," I say.

Normally, I don't get up this early, but Grandpa marched around the house tooting his bugle even before the sun got out of bed. Once Cocoa started wagging his tail, there was no chance I'd get back to sleep. He'd keep nudging me with his icy nose until I fed him and took him outside.

"You kids need to learn what a hard day's work is," Grandpa says. "Enough of this chocolate shop nonsense."

"The chocolate shop is not nonsense," Hannah says.

"Making chocolate is a hobby, like cooking or knitting," he says. "A real day's work gives you these." He curls up his arms and muscles pop. "You don't get big biceps by spooning chocolate onto cookie sheets."

"Mom would look weird with giant gorilla arms," I say.

"Plus, we don't spoon chocolate onto cookie sheets," Hannah says. "We ladle it into molds."

Grandpa waves his hand. "Whatever you do, it's not work."

"Neither is doing Revolutionary War reenactments," Hannah says.

Grandpa pokes at his fire with a stick. Embers crackle and his tin pot wobbles. "Reenactments are about understanding our past," he says.

"They're about sleeping in smelly tents with smelly people," Hannah says, holding her nose. "Pee-yew!"

Grandpa gives her a smiley squeeze and she giggles.

"I thought it was just a bunch of guys running around in a field with fake rifles," I say.

"They're called muskets and they're real," he says. "They just shoot blanks."

"Real?" Hannah says.

"When your parents get back from Glens Falls, I'm headed to Fort Ticonderoga for a reenactment. You two should come along and see for yourselves."

"Do we get muskets?" I ask.

"Yeah," Hannah says. "That might be fun."

"No muskets," Grandpa says, "but I do have a big surprise coming for you both. What do you think about that?"

I shrug and look down at my feet. Grandpa's idea of a surprise is probably different from mine. He gets excited about fancy brass buttons and animal pelts.

I hear the door slam. "We're headed out now," my father calls to us from the driveway. He's holding a stuffed-too-fat suitcase. "Stay out of trouble, you three."

Mom comes outside and stands behind me. She looks in the tin pot and wrinkles her nose just like Hannah did. "Hold down the fort for us," she says. "Miss Meredith is working the shop. Try not to bother her too much."

"Can we stop in for snacks?" Hannah asks.

Mom smiles and kisses both Hannah and me on the head. "Do you think I'm an ogre? Of course you can."

Mom and Dad make sure Grandpa knows all the right phone numbers and where every last thing is. They quiz him three or four times and then they're gone. Off to move us to dumb old Glens Falls.

Once Grandpa goes back to stirring his mush, I can't help but worry. When we move, all my friends, all my teachers, my whole school will be a hundred miles away. Plus, every time we go to Grandpa's it's the same. Every old lady hobbles out of her apartment and asks me to move a divan, an ottoman, or some other piece of furniture I've never heard the name of. And they pay with spare nickels, dusty cough drops, and cheek pinches.

I guess all that stuff wouldn't be the worst thing in the world, but the idea of losing Cocoa absolutely is. Just thinking about it gets my fists curled up into balls and my teeth all clenchy. Who would give him as much love as Hannah and me? This neighborhood is the only home Cocoa knows.

I huff out a steam engine breath and notice that Grandpa's head is slumped over and he's snoring like a chain saw. The fire is out and the mush has spilled over into the ashes.

I motion for Hannah to follow me. Good thing we're both wearing flip-flops because they slide off easily and make tiptoeing super silent. Even though I don't think dogs can tiptoe, Cocoa stays quiet, too. Not even he wants to try Grandpa's spiced-up Revolutionary War mush.

But if the idea of eating Grandpa's mush was bad, it's nothing compared to whom we run into out front.

"**Maybe** your family's chocolate would taste better if you shaved your dog and mixed his hair into the recipe."

Alan Kunkle, the son of the owners of Kunkle Kandies, is standing on our front walk. He's going into fifth grade with me, but he acts like he's in preschool. You know that saying about taking candy from a baby? I'll bet Alan Kunkle was the kid who did it.

Alan is not a dog-lick person, but Cocoa doesn't growl at him like I wish he would. Right now, I wish Cocoa had big, sharp fangs, a spiked collar, and a taste for eating snobby kids whose hair never gets messy. Instead, he sits quietly at my side. Not even my too-friendly dog wants to be friends with Alan Kunkle.

Alan pecks at his cell phone with his thumbs. "I heard you chickened out of the Chocolate Expo," he says. "Woulda been a waste of time anyway."

"You shut your big mouth!" Hannah barks, but before she has a chance to go on I step between them. An angry Hannah can be a dangerous thing.

Alan smirks. "You need an eight-year-old to fight your battles, Mason?"

"It's not a battle," I say.

"That's true," Alan says. "You need two sides for a battle. We've got a secret new creation that everyone is going to love. No competition."

Cocoa licks at Alan's elbow but I pull him back by his collar. I don't want my dog's tongue touching any part of Alan Kunkle. Cocoa starts racing around the yard. He bumps into the recycling bin. The blue folder for the Chocolate Expo is sitting right on top.

"It's okay to have two candy shops in town," I say. "People can come to us on Monday, Wednesday, and Friday, and they can come to you on Tuesday, Thursday, and Saturday."

Alan doesn't even smile. "Town*e* . . . Chocolate . . . Shop*pe* . . ." he says, pronouncing the silent letters at the ends of the words. "Can't your parents even spell? They got two out of three wrong."

"At least you can count," I say.

"It's a small-town thing," Hannah adds.

"That's your problem," Alan says. "Small-town folks don't understand business. My dad tells me running a chocolate shop is no different from running a huge company. You've got to get on top and stay there."

"The only thing you're on top of, Alan Kunkle, is a list of doofuses," Hannah mumbles.

"Mason! Hannah!" It's Grandpa Irving calling from the backyard. "Morning mush is ready. Get it while it's steaming!"

"Steaming mush?" Alan says. "What kind of weird, small-town family eats steaming mush?" He begins tapping at his cell phone again.

No matter how much I poke fun at my grandfather, when Alan pokes fun at him I want to poke that kid right in the eye.

But what I really want to do is beat the pants off his family's candy store. And that gets me thinking. What if Hannah and I could invent something really amazing for the

Chocolate Expo? My parents will be gone for a whole week. With my clueless, snoozing grandfather around and an entire chocolate laboratory downstairs, we have a good shot to prove that Towne Chocolate Shoppe is the place to buy chocolate treats for Valentine's Day, Easter, anniversaries, first dates, second dates, Arbor Day, International Talk Like a Pirate Day, and every other time people need chocolate.

I march over to the recycling bin and thrust my hand inside. Instead of the Chocolate Expo folder, I come up with a women's fashion magazine my mother threw out. The feature article is titled "50 Pairs of Scorching Heels Under $50."

"Is that your summer reading?" Alan says.

"No," I say. "I'm planning your outfit for the first day of school."

Alan scowls. His cell phone chirps and he turns away to check it.

I dig around the recycling bin some more, but the folder is gone. Hannah must have already grabbed it. I guess once in a while my pesky sister does something right.

Chapter 4

Crazy Concoctions

By the time Hannah and I set things up in the chocolate laboratory, it looks messier than I've ever seen it. Okay, maybe not as messy as when Cocoa goes on one of his rampages, but it's pretty bad.

We raided the storage closet, the pantry upstairs, and the leftovers from our Easter baskets for anything that might win awards inside a piece of chocolate. Piles of different possible fillings cover the countertops. Heaps of marshmallows tower over the gummy bears, who would probably run for avalanche cover if they could move their gummy little legs. The Sour Patch Kids would be crying for their mommies if they could see the stacks of Oreos threatening to topple onto them. And hopefully none of the animal crackers have nut allergies because the macadamias have already spilled onto them.

"I'm not so sure your parents would approve of you messing up the chocolate lab," Miss Meredith says from the stool behind the cash register.

"They said we could come down here as long as we didn't bug you," Hannah says.

It's not a lie, but it's definitely stretching the truth.

"Anyhow, Mom says that genius is one percent inspiration and ninety-nine percent 'mess-peration,'" I say. "By those numbers, we're almost finished."

"You're going to clean up when you're done, right?" Miss Meredith says.

"Of course," I say.

"Because I'm not your maid."

"We know," I say, trying to keep what Mom calls my "bad attitude voice" from sneaking in.

Miss Meredith looks up from her phone and peers over the low wall that separates the shop from the laboratory area. "Chocolate isn't cheap," she says. "Don't waste it or your parents will get upset."

"We're not wasting it," I say. This time my bad attitude voice does creep in.

"Anyhow," Hannah says, "Mom won't get upset when we invent the best chocolate ever and win the big Chocolate Expo."

"Is that what you're doing?" Miss Meredith says. "Well, good luck with that." Her cell phone chirps and she goes back to texting. The *clickety-clacking* of her falcon nails echoes so loud in my head that it's hard to think about chocolate or anything else.

I look at all the piled-up ingredients and tighten my grip on Cocoa's collar. He seems less itchy than he usually does around all this chocolate. Maybe he realizes how important what we're doing is.

"How come I get the feeling that inventing the best chocolate ever is going to be harder than we thought?" I say.

Hannah scans the counter. Her eyes dart back and forth between the mountains of fillings like she is solving some complicated math problem. "We just need to think of something no one else has thought of before," she says.

Cocoa stares at the graham crackers. He licks his tongue over his nose like he's trying to tell me something. Then he hops up and plants his front paws on the counter.

"Put Cocoa outside," Hannah says.

"Yeah, get the dog out of the store," Miss Meredith calls over.

I pull Cocoa back. "He's okay," I say. "He just needs to get used to it in here." I turn to Cocoa and stick my face right up to his. "Isn't that right, boy?"

Cocoa licks my nose. His tongue feels like a warm piece of bologna. But it's okay, I like bologna.

"If that dog messes things up, it's all of us who end up in the doghouse," Hannah says. "Me, you, *and* Cocoa."

"And me," Miss Meredith says. She snaps a photo of our mess.

Hannah glares over the wall at Miss Meredith.

Cocoa sits down and his tail starts thumping. His eyes don't leave that plate of graham crackers.

"What if we piled things on top of a graham cracker and covered it all in chocolate?" I say. Just the thought of it makes my taste buds wag their tails.

I snap a graham cracker in half and pile mini marshmallows, two Swedish fish, and three jelly beans on it. Then I place a caramel square on top. I grab the whole thing with a pair of tongs and dip it into a pot of melted milk chocolate. Two jelly beans shoot out the side and skitter across the counter, leaving a trail of yummy-looking chocolaty dots. I scoop the beans up and squish them back into my creation.

Hannah wrinkles her nose.

"What?" I ask her.

"That looks terrible."

"It's all my favorite candies piled together. How can it be bad?"

"Trust me," she says. "It'll be bad."

I take a bite. The still-steaming chocolate stings my lips and my arm jerks away from my face. My candy creation flings out of the tongs, flies across the lab, and splats against the far wall. Everything drops to the floor except the Swedish fish, who decide to stick there right above the drying racks. If they had mouths, they'd be making fun of me in Swedish.

"So?" Hannah asks.

"You were right," I say. "It was terrible."

She shoves me aside and gets to work.

Hannah checks the thermometer and adjusts the temperature of the melting pot. "It has to be one hundred and four degrees exactly or the chocolate gets grainy. And you can't stir it too much. That'll turn it grainy, too."

"What do you mean, grainy?" I say.

"Like sand," she says. "You wouldn't want to eat it."

"I'll be the judge of that."

Hannah pulls a pitcher of cream and a stick of butter from the refrigerator. "Tear off a piece of parchment paper," she says. "Lay it across the counter."

"Parchment paper?" I say. "Are we making chocolates or writing the Declaration of Independence?"

"It's for drying the chocolates, silly." She dumps more chocolate shavings into the melting pot. "Don't you pay attention to anything Mom does?"

"I'm her number one taste tester," I say. "Making the chocolates would ruin the magic of eating them."

Hannah rolls up her sleeves. "You're hopeless," she says.

"You're the hopeless one," I say back. But the truth is that I'm amazed by how much my third-grade sister knows about making chocolate. Of course, I'd never tell her that.

Just then, Grandpa Irving walks in. He's carrying a bundle wrapped in brown paper and tied with twine. "There you are!" he bellows. "Have I got a surprise for you."

He places his bundle on the countertop. It's about the size of an armadillo, which is a pet I've wanted ever since I wrote a report on them last year.

"Is the surprise for me or for Hannah?" I say.

"For both of you," he says.

Hannah and I eye the package suspiciously. Neither of us wants to be the first to move for it. The smell of melting chocolate fills the air and Cocoa begins sniffing and huffing. His eyes lock on the melting pot and I grab his collar more tightly.

"Go ahead," Grandpa says. "It won't bite."

Definitely not an armadillo. Too bad.

I snip the string around the package and

tear off the paper. The first thing I pull out is a white shirt that has more ruffles than a parade of princesses. Two heavy white stockings tumble out after it onto the counter.

I toss the clothes to Hannah. "These must be for you," I say.

Grandpa catches the clothes midair. "Don't be silly, Mason." He hands everything back to me. "These are for you. The height of fashion from 1776."

Hannah giggles. Cocoa puffs through his nose like he's laughing, too.

Grandpa paws through the rest of the clothing. He holds up a blue dress with strings crisscrossing the front and a white hat that looks like the top of a frosted-too-much cupcake. "Hannah, these are for you. If you're going to move in with me, the two of you should have your own Colonial clothing."

"We're going to a reenactment?" I ask.

"Why not?" Grandpa says. The excitement in his eyes keeps my mouth from telling him exactly why not.

"But *girls* wear stockings," I say. "Not boys."

"Back then, men and women both wore stockings," Grandpa says.

"And now, so do you," Hannah says to me, giggling some more.

Grandpa sorts through the rest of the clothing. "They go with these breeches," he says. "I had them made by a clothier who specializes in Colonial garb."

"A what who does what?" Hannah says.

"A guy who only makes clothes like this," I say.

"Oh," Hannah says. "A guy who makes stockings for boys."

We stand there, me holding my ruffled shirt, Hannah holding her poufy hat, and Cocoa hoping for a few graham crackers.

"Well?" Grandpa says, his eyebrows lifting up like two giant snowy caterpillars.

"Well what?" Hannah says.

Grandpa smiles. "What do you think?"

I open my mouth to thank him. Even though white stockings are the world's worst gift for a ten-year-old boy, my parents would want me to thank him. But before I have a chance to lie it starts to smell like my father left the coffee brewing too long.

"Something's burning," Miss Meredith calls to us.

"Oh no," Hannah says. "The chocolate!"

I look over her shoulder as she stirs the goop with a spoon. "Grainy?" I ask.

"Worse than grainy," she says. "Totally fried. We have to start over."

Just then, the phone rings. Hannah and I both leap for it, but it's my arm that knocks into the melting pot. Hot, gooey chocolate dumps out like a tidal wave and spills over the clothing Grandpa just gave us. And it gets even worse: My grip loosens on Cocoa's collar and he leaps up on his hind legs. His paws sweep through the chocolate and across the piles of ingredients. Gummy worms wriggle to the floor. Marshmallows tumble across the counter. Jelly beans clatter at my feet. Cocoa bounds around, leaving dark, smeary paw prints everywhere, including all over Hannah's shirt and hair. She stumbles back and her stirring spoon flings into the air, raining melted chocolate down on everything. It splatters the half of the lab that wasn't already splattered and makes yummy-looking drippy streaks on the walls, and the table, and even the ceiling.

"Grab the dog," Grandpa says.

"Get Cocoa out of here!" Hannah cries out.

But by the time I shove him outside, most of what we've collected to put inside our award-winning chocolate is either on the floor or tainted by Cocoa's turbo-sniffing snout.

Miss Meredith pulls her purse from under the counter. "I am so out of here," she says. "This place better be spotless and sparkling by tomorrow or I'm calling your parents."

Grandpa rolls up his sleeves. "Don't worry about that," he says. "Spotless and sparkling just happen to be my two middle names."

Chapter 6

All Washed Up

"**It's** no big deal." Grandpa kneels alongside the stream that runs behind our yard. He scrubs my ruffled shirt back and forth over a wooden washboard. "These clothes were made to take a beating. Most Colonial folks only had two outfits, one for work and one for Sunday. Clothes needed washing all the time."

Since he helped us clean the chocolate disaster, the least we can do is help Grandpa wash the clothes he bought for us. He tosses me a hunk of soap. Cocoa leaps at it as though it's a Frisbee. He lands in the stream and begins splashing through the water and chomping at the droplets midair.

Mom would be yelling for the dog to get out of the muddy water, but I figure this might be his last chance to play in the stream. Ever. If Cocoa wants to get muddy, that's fine by me.

"Try to scrub out the stains in those stockings," Grandpa tells me.

Hannah and I edge closer to the stream. I sit on a rock and begin working on cleaning an outfit I don't even want. Maybe I can scrub them to shreds.

"Who travels with a washboard in their car?" Hannah whispers to me as she piles the rest of the clothing at my feet. "Next thing you know we'll be making candles from animal fat instead of flicking on the lights."

"Or churning butter instead of opening up the refrigerator," I say.

"These are some stubborn stains," Grandpa says. I'm not sure if he hears what Hannah and I are saying, but he makes like he doesn't.

"Legend has it that George Washington insisted chocolate be given to every officer during the Revolution," he says.

"Really?" Hannah says.

"After the Colonists dumped all that tea in Boston Harbor, they needed something else to drink."

"I thought they drank coffee," I say. "That's what Mr. Hanchett told us in social studies."

"They did," Grandpa said. "Coffee wasn't taxed the same way tea was. But neither was chocolate. And back then chocolate was popular. Everyone wanted it."

"Everyone wants it now," Hannah says.

"Not *enough* people," I say, thinking about our shop.

Grandpa looks at the sudsy circle spreading into the stream. Once the bubbles drift from shore, the current sweeps them away in thin white streaks. "Back then, people thought chocolate had all sorts of uses," he says. "It kept you healthy and awake. It even made women fall in love with you."

"Like a love potion?" Hannah asks.

Grandpa smiles. "Just like a love potion."

"That can't be true," Hannah says. "We own a chocolate shop and no girl will come within a hundred yards of Mason."

My face gets steamy.

"Officers drank hot chocolate and chocolate wine," Grandpa says. He plants his hands on his hips like he's thinking about chocolate wine, but I can tell he's resting his back from all that bent-over scrubbing.

Hannah wrinkles her nose. "Chocolate wine sounds gross."

"I'm glad you think so," Grandpa says.

I look across the stream at the run-down mill. In school, we learned that the mill is the oldest building in town. That's saying a lot because all the buildings around here are old, even our house. Dad says the mill is a historical landmark, but no one has the money to restore it. Now, the roof is caving in and the water-wheel is mostly rotted away. I've even heard giant rats live in there.

But there is something worse than an old rotting-away, rat-filled mill across the stream. Alan Kunkle is sitting over there, too. The biggest rat of them all.

"What in the world are you doing?" he calls over.

"We're washing clothes the old-fashioned way," Grandpa says to him. "Why don't you come over and help out?"

Alan makes a crooked question mark with his face and laughs. My face gets steamier than before.

"No thanks," Alan says. He pulls out his phone and holds it up. "But I think I'll take a photo to share with our class. Real authentic, old-fashioned clothes washing. Classic."

"Classic it is!" Grandpa says, standing proudly beside his washboard. I look down and grit my teeth. If face steaminess had a dial, by now mine would be turned all the way up.

Then I hear a huge splash. I look up to see Cocoa standing on the stream bank where Alan Kunkle had been seconds ago. My dog's tongue is dangling from his mouth and he's giving me a proud look. Alan's sitting waist deep in the stream with a growly scowl on his face. The soapy water from Grandpa's washboard rushes over his legs.

Hannah bursts out laughing. "I was wrong," she says. "Doing laundry in the stream is a lot of fun!"

"That . . . dog . . ." Alan says, holding his cell phone high above his head. "That dog attacked me!"

"Oh hooey," Grandpa says. "That dog was only trying to be friendly. Now come over here and give us a hand."

Alan lifts himself out of the water. "Giving you a hand is the last thing I'd ever do!" He scrambles up the bank and disappears around the old mill.

Grandpa leans over his washboard and gets back to work on my ruffled shirt. "I'm not sure who that boy is," he says, "but he has some serious issues."

"You don't know the half of it," I say.

Chapter 7

Masterpiece in Pieces

"They look amazing," I tell Hannah, looking at the row of chocolates drying on the parchment paper. "What's in them?"

"I took your graham cracker idea and topped it with molten marshmallows and a hint of caramel. Then I enrobed it in milk chocolate with dark and white chocolate drizzles." Even with the smudges of chocolate across her face, Hannah seems super fancy with all those words I've never heard coming out of her mouth.

"It's a chocolate-covered s'more!" I say.

"I had to use the last of Mom's chocolate," Hannah says, "but who wouldn't put a ribbon on something like this?"

"Everyone loves s'mores," I say. "Everyone with a heartbeat, at least."

Hannah beams.

"But it's still missing something," she says. "I tasted one and it feels like it could use an extra twist."

I lean in and take a deep breath. The scent of warm chocolate fills my head. "I wonder . . ."

"Don't you touch my chocolates," Hannah warns me.

"I won't," I say. "They're tiny works of art. But I wonder if a dash of sea salt might make them better."

"Salt? On a s'more?"

"You know, kind of like the salty chocolate-covered pretzels Mom makes. We could combine two perfect ideas."

Hannah thinks for a moment, then nods. "Let's try it out."

She dusts one chocolate-covered caramel s'more with sea salt and cuts it in half. I snatch up mine and pop it into my mouth.

The chocolate begins to melt over my tongue and a warm feeling spreads through me, like nothing in the world could be wrong. Soon the caramel and marshmallow remind me they are there, sweet like the rest, but filling a different part of me that the chocolate couldn't find. Then the salt perks up and my whole face tingles. My eyes roll so far back that I can practically see my brain.

"That is amazing," I say. "I mean really incredible."

"Salt was the perfect touch," Hannah says. She gets to work sprinkling the rest of the chocolates.

"What are you making?" Miss Meredith says from the front of the shop.

When we tell her, her eyebrows go up in surprise. "Sounds yummy," she says. "Can I have a taste?"

"After we're finished," Hannah says. "One each. We need to save the rest for the Chocolate Expo."

Miss Meredith whips out her cell phone and starts pecking.

No matter how badly I feel about it, it was a good idea to lock Cocoa in his crate. Without having to worry about him going choco-crazy, Hannah was able to focus on work. *Get this, get that, get some other thing I've never heard of.* She barked orders at me like a general might bark at a bunch of soldiers. With Cocoa safely away, I could even focus on my sea salt idea. With the big tray of soon-to-be-award-winning chocolates sitting in front of us, I can't complain.

"The judges are going to love these," Hannah says.

"How can they not?" I say.

The bell over the front door jingles. It's Mrs. Davis. Her arms are loaded with grocery bags. "I need a small box of nut clusters," she says to Meredith. "I have my book club tonight and – WHOOPS!"

It's not just the "Whoops" that grabs my attention. Even weighed down with all those bags, Mrs. Davis's arms fly right into the air. I can't see below her waist because of the low wall between the chocolate lab and the shop, but it looks like something (or someone) shot past her legs.

It doesn't take a hiccup's time to realize it's Cocoa. *But how did he get back in here?* I wonder as he barrels past Mrs. Davis and zips around the shop in loopy circles. He knocks over two towers of chocolate pralines and the chocolate mint wafers display. Miss Meredith tries to grab him, but Cocoa darts between her feet and charges back into the lab. I snag his collar, but he spins around and swipes his slobbery bologna tongue across my ear. It tickles so much that I can't help but let go.

Cocoa scrambles around a few more times, overturning boxes and knocking over a rack of chocolate molds. Hannah lunges at him, but that only gets Cocoa thinking we're playing tag. Before I can grab hold of his collar again, he starts racing around the kitchen. He knocks every pot and pan onto the tile and bangs into the table, sending a basket of utensils crashing down. Finally, Cocoa leaps like an Olympic track star and lands on top of Hannah's chocolate-covered salty s'mores. He plows the parchment paper and the chocolates to the floor in a dog-hairy, chocolate-covered, salty, crinkled mess.

"You said you put him in his crate!" Hannah cries.

"I did," I say, chasing Cocoa around the worktable. Metal bowls crash to the tile louder than cymbals at a rock concert. "I double-checked the latch, too!"

Cocoa skids around and slams into the wall. Paneling splits and a piece of molding falls down. He takes another few laps, then stops to sniff at a box of caramels. When I finally grab him and catch my breath, I have a look around. The store looks like it was shaken up inside a giant snow globe. Cocoa gives a puff of breath and licks my chin.

"That . . . dog . . ." Miss Meredith says, her voice shaky. Dark chocolate drips down her forehead. She yanks off her apron and tosses it on the counter. "I refuse to do this anymore. I quit."

I can't be sure, but as she turns to leave I think I see a smile peek at me from one little corner of her mouth. By the time I have a chance to get a second look, the door has already jingled shut behind her.

Mrs. Davis is still standing there, her box of nut clusters in her hand. "I'd offer to help," she says, "but my book club starts in twenty minutes. I'll just put the money next to the cash register. Keep the change."

After she leaves, I turn to Hannah. "What are we going to do?" I say. "Mom and Dad are going to get steamier than steamed milk."

"It's me who's angry," Hannah says. "I put in all the hard work."

"I'm sure that cage was locked," I say.

"You say that every time."

"But this time I mean it!"

Hannah picks up the parchment paper. Half the chocolates slide off onto the floor. All of them are crushed into a gooey mess. "You blew it, Mason. You blew it big-time."

Tears fill my eyes and I look away.

That's when I see it. Past the wreckage of the kitchen. Beyond the mess of broken paneling and fallen molding. It's there. Clear as day. Where the wall used to be, I see a secret room.

"Wait!" I say to Hannah. "Look over here."

I pull away the busted paneling and peer into the darkness. It's dusty, musty, and stuffy in there. All three, but mostly that first one.

"Stop, Mason. It's over. We don't have any chocolate left. I used the last of it on the salty caramel s'mores."

"But there's a bunch of stuff in here," I say. "Old stuff."

And it's true. I see an iron skillet, a basket bigger than a sombrero, and a heavy-looking bowl with an even-heavier-looking stone stick in it. Deeper in the cramped room I see something that looks like a metal block and a big metal rolling pin.

Hannah looks over my shoulder. "What is all that junk?" she says.

"I don't know," I say. "Help me pull it out."

Hannah clears some space while I creep into the secret room. It's dark but I can see old floorboards and beams inside the walls.

I start handing things out to Hannah.

"What do you think all this stuff is?" she says. "Maybe Mr. Perkins at the antiques shop would buy it."

I poke my head out of the secret room and brush a cobweb from my eyes. "What do you think it's all worth?"

"Not enough to save this place," she says. "Most of it looks like it should be in the junkyard."

"That's what people like about antiques," I say. "The crustier the better. I saw an antiques show on television once. The crusty stuff is called patina."

Hannah shakes the skillet. Crumbly dirt falls from it. "Not this crusty," she says, wrinkling her nose. "No one wants creepy haunted house stuff."

I go back into the secret room and tug on the metal block. It's heavier than it looks, and that's saying a lot because the thing is as big as an anchor. I heave on it and it budges an inch. Another tug scooches it an inch farther. Finally, I give my mightiest pull. My back strains and my shoulders burn. That's when my grip gives out. I tumble back against the inside of the wall and my head hits a beam. Dust showers down on my face and I start to cough.

"Are you okay?" Hannah asks.

Cocoa inches forward and whines a little.

"Just a little bump," I say.

"That's what you get, then," she says.

"For what?"

"For not locking Cocoa's cage while we were working," Hannah says. "Mom calls it 'just desserts.' "

I want to tell her that I did latch the cage. I remember the slider sticking a little as I pushed it closed. I even double-checked that the door was shut tight, then triple-checked.

The door jingles. "There you are!" Grandpa bellows. "I saw that Meredith girl charge off like a cavalry horse. I figured I'd better get down here to see what trouble you two have gotten into." Then he sees the damage. "Whoa" is all he says.

"It wasn't us," Hannah says. "It was Cocoa."

Grandpa smiles so big that his caterpillar

eyebrows almost kiss. "I'll help you get this place cleaned up after dinner," he says. "I've got some venison stew over the fire."

"Venison?" I say. "Where did you get venison?"

"At the farmers' market," he says. "They have the freshest foods and everything is one-hundred-percent organic. I'm using the same recipe George Washington served during that cold winter at Valley Forge."

"Isn't venison deer meat?" Hannah says. "I'm not eating Bambi."

"Suit yourself," Grandpa says. "I'll whip up some more of my mush."

Hannah grumbles.

Grandpa crouches down and looks in at me. "So, Mason, are you building an addition to the house?"

"Cocoa discovered a secret room," I say.

"Well, that dog is a regular Christopher Columbus," he says, which makes Hannah giggle. "Now, bring that fancy book of yours upstairs and get washed up."

"What book?" I ask.

"The book you're leaning on," Grandpa says.

I look down and see a dark red leather cover under my hand. It's caked in haunted house patina and covered with crumbled pieces of wall. I scoop it up and flip it open. It's some sort of old journal book. On the first page in fancy handwriting it says:

Beatrice Cabot Family Recipes

1763

I turn the page, then I turn a few more.

"What is it?" Hannah asks, trying to peer over the top of the book.

"Hannah," I say. "I think our problems are solved."

Chapter 9

A New Recipe

"Mom's family has lived in this house for a billion years," I say. "This Beatrice Cabot lady must have been our Great-Great-Great-Great-(however-many-times)-grandmother."

Wearing Mom's apron, Grandpa looks like a bouquet of flowers, but he doesn't seem to notice. He places three filled-to-the-brim bowls on the table, one for each of us. Then he places another on the floor for Cocoa. As expected, Hannah wrinkles her nose.

"So all of those old things we found . . ." Hannah says.

I move my book aside so I won't drip Bambi juice on it. I flip through a few pages. Great-Great-Great-(however-many-times)-Grandma Cabot kept detailed notes about cooking. She listed recipes and utensils and her favorite ways to keep a fire lit through the winter. She even drew pictures of how to best trap and butcher a rabbit. That last one gets Hannah to wrinkle up her nose more than ever.

The too-incredible-to-be-believed part is that she wrote a whole long section about making chocolate and drew sketches to show each step. "It looks like all that stuff we found is chocolate-making equipment from the old days," I say.

Grandpa sits down beside me. The ruffles on his apron brush my arm. "Old-time chocolate making," he says. "Now, that's something I'd like to see."

"I'd like to see you wear that apron to the supermarket," I say.

Hannah giggles and picks through her stew with her spoon. She scoops up a chunk of carrot and nibbles on it. "Is it hard to make chocolate from scratch?" she asks.

"I'm sure it wasn't easy," Grandpa says. "Nothing was back then."

"We should clean off all that stuff and give it a try," Hannah says. "What ingredients do we need?"

I taste the stew. It's not bad once you stop thinking about Bambi. I can imagine a Revolutionary War soldier really warming up to a bowl of this stuff after a long day of marching through the snow. "There are a few chocolate recipes in here," I say. "I've never even heard of some of these ingredients."

Grandpa puts on his glasses and looks at the book. "We can get most of these things at the farmers' market," he says. "Not sure about the cocoa beans, though."

At the sound of his name, Cocoa perks his head up from his bowl. He is doing the exact opposite of Hannah, only eating the meat from his stew. The carrots and peas plunk from his mouth with a flick of his bologna tongue.

I eat another spoonful of the stew when the computer in the family room chimes. Hannah bolts from the table. "That's Mom and Dad!" she cries out.

I don't know why she's in such a rush to video chat with them. I'm sure they've already heard the bad news from Miss Meredith.

Hannah flicks on the monitor and sits down. "Mom, Dad!" she says. "You need to come home right away. You won't believe what we found!"

My parents' heads are squished together on the screen like a peanut cluster. "Hannah," Mom says in her I'm-not-kidding-around voice. "Where's Mason? Get him over here."

I slide out of my seat and stand behind my sister.

"How could you let Cocoa into the store again?" Mom says. "Meredith told me it's happened twice since we've left. Twice!"

"This carelessness has got to stop," Dad says.

I open my mouth to explain, but my dad goes on. "We left you in charge of the shop and now Meredith is gone. What are we going to do now?"

I'm not sure if this is one of those don't-answer-it-or-you'll-be-in-big-fat-trouble questions, so I keep quiet.

That gives Mom a chance to jump in.

And she does. She talks about responsibility and my carelessness until Dad tags in again. They go back and forth like that for a few minutes until finally Grandpa picks up the computer mouse. He starts talking into it like it's a microphone. "Bill, Loretta, don't worry. I've got everything under control."

My parents both chuckle at the sight of Grandpa, but they nudge each other and get serious again.

"I'll work in the store until you get back." Grandpa talks slowly and loudly like they might not be able to hear him. "We don't need that Meredith girl. I can spot bad eggs from a country mile."

"You can't do all that work," Mom says. "Just restacking the boxes —"

"The kids will help," Grandpa says. "A hard day's work will be good for them."

"I don't know . . ." Mom says.

"Trust me," Grandpa says.

But looking at him in his flowery apron talking into the computer mouse, I'm not so sure they should trust him to tie his shoes, let alone run a chocolate shop — even one that's about to close forever.

Chapter 10

Back in Business

"**Pshaw,**" Grandpa says, straightening the last pile of boxes on the counter. "Running a chocolate shop is child's play."

"We *are* children," Hannah says.

Grandpa ignores Hannah's very good point. "A real day's work is digging ditches or working in a mine."

"When was the last time you worked in a mine?" I ask him.

Grandpa smiles a little. "Never you mind that," he says.

"Mom told me you were an accountant before you retired," I say.

"I said never you mind."

It takes us a few hours, but the store is finally spotless and sparkling again. With Cocoa double-locked in his crate, we're able to work without any trouble. The pots and pans are on their racks. The utensils are in their places. The entire front of the shop doesn't look like a tornado twisted through here anymore. The only difference now is the hole in the wall and the old equipment sitting in the middle of the chocolate lab.

"Are you sure you cleaned that stuff up?" I ask Hannah.

"Look at it," Hannah says. "It's practically gleaming."

I wouldn't use the word *gleaming* but instead of a bunch of crusty, crumbly pieces of junk we pulled out of a crusty, crumbly secret room, now the chocolate-making equipment looks usable. Used, but usable. The heavy bowl and stone stick (which Grandpa told me were called a mortar and pestle) are smooth and ready to grind cocoa beans. The roller and metal block (which I found out from Beatrice Cabot's book is called a chocolate stone) are clean and shiny. Even the skillet (which I already knew the name of) looks good.

The bell over the door jingles. It's Mrs. McEneny. She runs the farmers' market in town. She's holding a loaded-to-the-brim tote bag in one hand and a water bottle filled with goopy green liquid in the other.

"Rachel!" Grandpa says to her. "Right on time."

"A promise is a promise," Mrs. McEneny says. She takes a swig from her bottle. Whatever she's drinking doesn't look very good.

Grandpa reaches under the counter and pulls out an assortment of boxes. He slides it all to Mrs. McEneny.

"Just like we agreed," Grandpa says. "An even trade. A hundred dollars in ingredients for a hundred dollars in chocolates."

"I love trading with local businesses," Mrs. McEneny says. "Especially when that local business is a chocolate shop." She looks at Hannah and me and winks. Then she takes another sip from her bottle.

"Mrs. McEneny," Hannah says. "What are you drinking?"

"It's a wheatgrass, flaxseed, and pomegranate smoothie," she says. "It's packed with vitamins and antioxidants."

"That sounds awful," Grandpa says.

"Actually, George Washington drank them

during the hot summers in Virginia. They were quite popular back then."

"Really?" Grandpa says.

"Of course not," Mrs. McEneny says. "But if he did, maybe he wouldn't have had all those wooden teeth." She shakes Grandpa's hand. "Let me know if you want to work out a trade again."

After she leaves, Grandpa brings us the tote bag.

"What is all that stuff?" I ask him.

"It's all the ingredients you need to make your first batch of Colonial-era chocolate. Cocoa beans, sugar, anise, vanilla, nutmeg, cinnamon, even orange rind. I found the recipe in Beatrice Cabot's book. I'll run the store. You guys get to work." He places the folder for the Chocolate Expo on the counter. "You have three days until the big event. Then you have some ribbons to win."

. . .

Making Colonial chocolate is a lot harder than making regular chocolate. With regular chocolates, you melt already-made chocolate in a pot and dip things into it. With Colonial chocolate, you have to make everything from scratch. We take triple-quadruple-extra care to follow the directions exactly.

First Grandpa helps us roast the cocoa beans in the skillet. Too much and they burn. Not enough and the shells don't crackle off. Then you have to go outside and toss the beans around in the basket. That gets most of the little pieces of shell to drift away on the breeze. Cocoa likes that part. He jumps in the air and nips at the fluttery specks.

Once that's done, the real work begins. You need to grind the little pieces of cocoa beans with the mortar and pestle, then on the grinding stone with the roller. That part is hard, but Grandpa loves working that roller up and down until the beans turn into drippy, slippy goo. He says doing that job might be *harder* than working in a mine!

Then you add sugar and the rest of the spices in just the right amounts and grind it all over again until everything is mixed up and smooth.

From there, Hannah takes over. She's decided that good Colonial-era chocolate deserves to meet the world in a good Colonial-era way. Back then people didn't eat chocolate the way we do. Kids didn't eat chocolate bars. There were no candy shops like ours where we're always struggling to make the most interesting and yummy treats. People bought chocolate in big hunks from a chocolate maker and, like Grandpa told us, they melted it into drinks.

Hannah took our chocolate and poured it into a long rectangular pan. That way, she said, we can cut it off by the inch like Great-Great-Great-(however-many-times)-Grandma Beatrice.

The best part about it all is that not once did Alan Kunkle poke his head into our store, around our yard, or even across the stream. It's amazing how much a kid can relax when he knows he doesn't have a camera staring at him every second.

It takes a lot of time to get it right, but by the night before the Chocolate Expo we're ready. The blocks of chocolate are wrapped in parchment paper. The banner we made is rolled up next to the door. And even though she might not approve, Mom's fancy tablecloth is ready.

"Only one more detail to work out," Grandpa says as Hannah and I brush our teeth before bed.

"What's that?" I say, toothpaste drool dripping down my wrist.

Grandpa whips out those Colonial outfits he bought us. "Time to gear up in ruffles and white stockings," he says.

Hannah laughs so hard toothpaste splatters out of her mouth.

"No way," I say.

"Way," Hannah says. "If we're going to win the Chocolate Expo, we have to give it everything we've got. Those outfits are perfect."

Grandpa levels his eyes at me. "Way" is all he says.

Chapter 11

The Big Event!

The best thing about owning a chocolate shop is all the chocolate. That might sound obvious, but a girl in my class, Lindsey Ling, told me something interesting. Her family owns Slippy Slide Water Park outside of town and she once said that she is bored with waterslides. Bored with them! All the free watersliding she could ever want and she never puts on her bathing suit anymore.

That would never happen to me with chocolate. There is something magical about the way it slowly melts on your tongue, the way just a little bit of it fills your whole mouth and makes every one of your taste buds jump for joy. Even the smell of it sends a warm feeling flowing through your body. No, chocolate and I are going to be buddies forever, no matter what.

So, standing in the middle of a big room filled with chocolate is just about the most incredible thing I can think of. Of course, standing in the middle of a big room filled with chocolate while dressed as a Colonial fool sort of spoils it. Part of me wants to play with the fountain gushing chocolate like a waterfall, down, down, down into a giant bowl where people can dunk marshmallows, bananas, and cake on the ends of sticks. The rest of me wants to hide behind our display where Hannah is handing out free samples.

Our banner reads:

Towne Chocolate Shoppe
Yankee Doodle Candy

"Taste How Sweet History Can Be!"

Grandpa said we couldn't bring the skillet or the winnowing basket for our demonstration today. The first would be a fire hazard and the second would make a dusty mess. He did let us bring the chocolate stone and the roller, though. Grandpa is working them like a pro, and it's bringing people to our table like baby goats during feeding time at the petting zoo.

"Do you have any more samples?" I call over to Hannah.

"I'm cutting the chocolate as fast as I can!" she says.

But no matter how quickly I lay out the tiny napkins and how quickly Hannah cuts up the blocks, our chocolate disappears.

"Looks like you two are doing all right," Grandpa says. He scoops the syrupy brown goo onto a piece of waxed paper and loads the stone with more crushed cocoa beans. His sleeves are rolled up and his forearms bulge like he's been doing this his whole life.

"The judges haven't come around yet," I say, handing a sample to a young couple pushing a baby stroller. "We'll see how we do then."

Click!

I hear the sound of a camera phone. My shoulders tighten up and I turn around.

Alan Kunkle. He finishes keying something into his phone.

"Nice outfit, Mason," Alan says. "I'm sure

our social studies class will love to see your tight pants and stockings."

"They're called breeches," I say. "They're no different than baseball pants."

"They're way different," Alan says.

Something chirps in Hannah's pocket. Her head jerks up and she scowls. "Ignore him," she says. "He's just jealous we're doing so well."

"Jealous?" Alan says. "Why would I be jealous?"

"Because our chocolate is better than anything that your giant blinking monster machine can spit out," Hannah says.

"I'm not sure that matters much," Alan says. "My mom —"

But he never gets to finish his sentence because the judges arrive. There are three of them: two ladies and a man. The larger of the two women, the one with the jiggly Jell-O neck and makeup that looks like it was put on by blindfolded monkeys, is Mrs. Kunkle. She is the most opposite thing from a dog-lick person I've ever seen.

Mrs. Kunkle looks back and forth between her son and me. "Who is your little friend, Alan?"

"Mason's not my friend," he says. "He's just some kid from school."

"Let's not be rude," Mrs. Kunkle says. She puts on her glasses and reads our sign. "Just because their store is having troubles . . ."

"But —"

"I said let's not be rude, Alan. Now, go back to the booth. We've already judged our family's chocolates. We've won top prize for our chocolate-covered caramel sea salt s'mores."

"Hey, that's my recipe!" Hannah says.

"Yeah, we invented that," I say.

"Nonsense, it was Alan's idea," Mrs. Kunkle says. She turns to her son. "Your father is organizing our ribbons and trophies. Why don't you go give him a hand?"

Alan disappears into the crowd.

"They already got ribbons and trophies?" Hannah asks. "You haven't even tried our chocolates yet."

Mrs. Kunkle looks down her nose at Hannah as though she is some sort of swamp rat. "What are you implying, young lady?"

"Nothing, I guess," Hannah says. She places three samples on a small platter and hands it to Mrs. Kunkle. "We made chocolate using authentic techniques handed down through our family." She goes on to tell the judges about the antique equipment we found and the recipe used by Great-Great-Great-(however-many-times)-Grandma Beatrice.

The judges let her finish and Mrs. Kunkle speaks first. "I'm afraid I can't permit these samples into the competition," she says. She gestures to the grinding stone and roller Grandpa is using. "That equipment looks unsanitary. I'm concerned for the well-being of the judges as well as our visitors."

A gasp spreads through the crowd and Grandpa steps forward. "Now, just wait one second here," he says, waggling his chocolate roller. "These kids have worked their tail feathers off for this competition. I'm not going to let you waltz in here and take it all away without giving them a chance."

Mrs. Kunkle purses her lips into a polite smile-that's-not-really-a-smile. "I'm afraid you have no say in the matter."

"But I do," the man judge says. "There are three of us, Shirley. Just because Kunkle Kandies sponsored the expo doesn't mean you get to run the show."

"Kunkle Kandies sponsored the expo?" Hannah mutters. "How is that fair?"

"There are three judges, Walter," Mrs. Kunkle says. "As long as two of us agree to disqualify them, there is nothing you can do about it." She glares down at the third judge. "I'm sure you're in agreement with me. Aren't you, Danielle?"

The lady named Danielle squirms a little. She's much younger than Mrs. Kunkle, and much smaller. She looks at the chocolate samples, then at Mrs. Kunkle. "Actually, I'd like to give it a try," she finally says.

That's when the doors to the auditorium burst open and Cocoa charges in.

Chapter 12

Cocoa Catastrophe

"**Get** . . . ! That . . . ! Dog . . . !" Mrs. Kunkle screams.

The crowd scrambles as Cocoa starts destroying the Chocolate Expo. His nails skitter on the polished-to-a-shine floor and he slides into one table after another. He sends a display of chocolate-dipped strawberries tumbling. He topples the chocolate-covered Oreo table. People start chasing Cocoa to save their own displays, and guests start running away to avoid getting trampled.

Chocolate Labs are not known for their strength or their speed, but Cocoa is proving anyone who ever believed those things one hundred percent wrong.

"It's not his fault!" I cry out. "He's just like the rest of us! He loves the smell of chocolate!"

"That dog is *not* just like the rest of us," Mrs. Kunkle barks as she charges past. Her Jell-O neck jiggles. "That dog is a nuisance. He is a nuisance and a terror!"

I want to defend Cocoa, but right now is probably not the best time.

Cocoa slams into our display. His eyes are wide and his tongue hangs from his smiling mouth. I scoop up the last tray of chocolate just as it slides to the edge of the table. Hannah moves alongside me.

"I guess no ribbons for us, huh?" she says.

"I guess not."

"How're we going to stop Cocoa?" she asks.

"Stopping Cocoa right now would be like stopping a hurricane," I say.

Cocoa skitters past again. This time, two security guards are chasing him.

"Hey," Hannah says. "Look over there."

I follow her pointing finger. Standing by the open door — holding it open, actually — is Alan Kunkle. He's got a huge smile across his face. He trots over to his mother and joins the chase.

"Do you think Alan did this?" I ask Hannah.

"I'm sure of it," Hannah says. She pats her pocket. "I have proof."

"What do you mean you have —" But before I can finish my sentence a scream rises up and an elephant spray of melted chocolate flings into the air. When the crowd clears, laughter rings out. On the floor in the middle of the auditorium sit Mrs. Kunkle and Alan. I barely recognize them. They are completely covered in melted chocolate from the overturned fountain. I think taking a bath in chocolate would be fun, but Mrs. Kunkle does not share my feeling.

"Disqualified!" she yells out. "Disqualified!" She tries to stand up, but she slips in the dark liquid and starts flopping on the floor. "Someone call Animal Control. Have that beast removed from my event!"

"Cocoa is not a beast!" It's a voice I haven't heard in days, at least not in person. I turn to see my father at the entrance to the Chocolate Expo. Mom is standing alongside him. "He's our pet."

At the sound of Dad's voice, Cocoa stops. He trots alongside my father and sits down. As fast as the hurricane started, it ends.

Soon, Animal Control officers show up. They explain to my parents that Cocoa needs to be held until they make sure he's had all of his shots and that he didn't cause any serious injuries.

I explain that Cocoa would never hurt anyone on purpose, but they still take him away. As the lock slides into place and I see them wheel Cocoa out to the truck, I can't help the tears from streaming down my face.

"What are we going to do?" I say.

Mom and Dad give Hannah and me big hugs. Usually, those hugs are really good at making me feel better, but this time it doesn't work.

"We'll figure something out," Mom says. "But maybe this is all for the best."

"What do you mean?" Hannah says.

Dad kneels down. "We're moving," he says. "Your new school starts in two weeks. We can't take Cocoa with us. Maybe the shelter can find him a good home, one where he doesn't have to smell chocolate and go crazy all the time."

"But *everyone* goes crazy for chocolate," I say between sniffles. "He's just behaving like the rest of us want to behave."

Dad smiles, but I can tell it's just to cover up his frown. "I wish it were that easy," he says. "Maybe we can help Cocoa find a better home. Sometimes life is about finding the right situation at the right time."

And that gives me an idea.

"The right time," I say.

"What?" Mom says.

I brighten. "The right time. That's our problem. We have the best chocolate," I say, looking over at Grandpa, "but not the best chocolate for today. We have the best chocolate for 1776."

"I don't understand," Dad says.

Grandpa waggles his chocolate roller. "I think I do," he says. "Let me make a few phone calls."

Chapter 13

The Right Time

A cannon booms on top of the stone wall behind us. Smoke poofs into the sky and people cheer. There are a bunch of battle reenactments through the weekend, but they load and fire that cannon every hour. I wish they would give us some sort of warning, though. That thing is LOUD!

Mom and Dad scraped together every dollar they could and bought a ton of ingredients. Mrs. McEneny at the farmers' market gave them a discount in exchange for a part of each batch of our Yankee Doodle Candy chocolate.

She likes it so much that she wants to sell it right at the market!

Grandpa is still doing his favorite job: working the roller over the grinding stone. Mom is roasting the cocoa beans over the campfire and Hannah is tossing the cracked beans into the air in the winnowing basket. When there's a breeze, you've got to watch out not to breathe in all the dust flittering around. My job is grinding up the nibs with the mortar and pestle, and Dad is taking care of the money. Even Cocoa helps. He prances around in the tricorn hat and ruffled collar Grandpa had specially made for him. Cocoa even brought a customer to our booth by tugging on a woman's dress.

It's as though making chocolate the old-fashioned way is a perfect fit for our family. Everyone has his or her own job!

And, of course, we're all wearing Colonial clothing. The great thing is that since everyone else is dressed like this I don't feel weird at all. Stockings, frills, breeches, it doesn't matter.

There are tons of different booths here, all with people in outfits like ours. To our left sits a woman weaving baskets and a guy who sells dried meats. A bearded man is tanning hides behind us. Boy, is that a smelly job. It makes me glad we make chocolate.

"This was a great solution," Mom says as she wraps a block of chocolate in paper and hands it to an old woman.

"Yeah, Mason," Dad says. "It's one of the most basic ideas in business. If you can't do well in your old market, find a new one."

"Plus, this is more fun," Hannah says. "It's one thing to melt chocolates and dip stuff into it. But making chocolate from scratch is a whole different thing. The Kunkles have nothing on us."

Dad hands a man his change and stuffs cash into his already-stuffed pouch. "And the good news is that we're making enough money to give this new business a try."

"You mean we get to stay in our house?" I say.

"And at our school?" Hannah adds.

"For now," Mom says. "We'll see how things go."

I look down at Cocoa. He is lapping water from a wooden bowl (Grandpa told us we need to keep everything as Colonial as possible). As always, he slurps three tonguefuls, then takes a breath before he goes back for more.

"What about Cocoa?" I ask.

Cocoa lifts his head to look at us, then goes back to his water.

"Mason," Dad says. "Cocoa can't control himself."

Mom jiggles her skillet. The cocoa beans pop and crackle. "He's caused so much trouble."

"I know," I say, "but if he hadn't caused so much trouble, we never would have found the secret room with the chocolate-making equipment and Great-Great-Great-(however-many-times)-Grandma Beatrice's chocolate recipes. When you think about it, Cocoa sort of saved us."

Mom squiggles her lips and looks at Dad. They make uggy-buggy eyes at each other.

"That pet of yours . . ." Dad says.

"Cocoa is not a pet," I say. "He is a member of our family."

Dad starts to shake his head.

"Come on already," Grandpa says. "You can't take a dog away from two little kids. You guys make worse decisions than General Howe during his 1777 Saratoga campaign!"

Mom sighs. "I guess Cocoa can stay," she finally says.

"But, Mason, you're in charge of him," Dad adds. "No more letting him storm into the chocolate shop."

"I promise," I say.

"Me, too!" Hannah says.

We both rush to Cocoa and give him hugs and belly rubs. Cocoa rolls on his back and starts kicking his leg. I'm not sure he understands what just happened, but I can tell he's happy.

"Now, let's get back to work," Grandpa says.

Before long, we're almost sold out. I mean, who can say no to authentic Colonial chocolate at an authentic American Revolution reenactment? The huge mountain we started with is down to a few paper-wrapped pieces and two small blocks. Mom is cutting those up and wrapping them while Dad and Grandpa sit on a wooden bench counting the money.

"Why don't you two wander around a bit?" Mom says.

"Have a look at the reenactment down on the hill," Grandpa adds. "The Patriots are about to beat the pants off General Burgoyne."

"It's britches, not pants," I say. "Anyhow, I thought the British won at Fort Ticonderoga in 1777."

Grandpa smiles. "See, I've taught you something after all."

As we walk away, I hear Grandpa talking to Dad. "So, I was thinking about that mill across the stream from your house . . ."

"What about it?" Dad says.

"If we fix it up, we can get it grinding cocoa

beans all day. We'll expand production and start shipping to reenactments all over the country."

Dad laughs. "Let's not get too hasty, Pops. Right now, it's one batch at a time."

Hannah and I walk around the huge stone wall and make our way along the path. As soon as we see the Redcoats, it's like we've been transported back in time. A long line of British soldiers marches across a field while Patriots squat behind trees and boulders with their muskets. The cannon booms and the battle begins.

"You two look more ridiculous than ever," a voice says.

Alan Kunkle. Is that kid everywhere?

He takes a photo of us.

I try to ignore him, but he goes on. "You couldn't compete with real chocolate geniuses so you had to come here, huh?"

Something chirps in the folds of Hannah's dress and she smiles.

"ALAN!" It's Mr. Kunkle. He stomps over. "Just because you invented the award-winning chocolate for the expo doesn't mean you don't have to pay attention. Last marking period's social studies grade is riding on this report you're going to write. Mr. Hanchett was kind enough to offer you extra credit. Now, don't blow it."

Alan's face goes red. "You tell anyone about this, Mason, and I'll show everyone the photos of you in that outfit."

"I don't care what you show people," I say. "I like this outfit."

"Yeah," Hannah says, straightening her bonnet. "And your days of being a chocolate genius are over."

"What are you talking about?" Alan says.

Hannah pulls out a small, black rectangle. The glassy front glints in the sun.

"What's that?" Alan says.

"It's Miss Meredith's cell phone," she says. "She's your cousin! She was texting you our recipes for months before she quit. Plus, she was telling you when to let Cocoa out of his crate. It was you all along!"

"That's a lie," Alan says.

"I've seen all the texts so don't deny it," Hannah says, tossing the phone to Alan. "I even printed them out. She calls you Boo-Boo."

Alan scowls and stuffs Miss Meredith's phone into his pocket.

Just then, amid all the musket fire, Cocoa charges out onto the battlefield in his tricorn hat and ruffled collar. He bounds past the Patriots and begins darting around the Redcoats as though they were an obstacle course. Then, without slowing down, he leaps at the man playing British Major General John Burgoyne. General Burgoyne falls onto his back and Cocoa starts licking his face over and over.

Hannah runs out after Cocoa. "I don't think this is how it actually happened," she says.

I chase after Hannah, laughing. "Somehow, I think you're right," I say. "I just hope General Burgoyne is the kind of general who likes dog licks!"

• About the Author •

ERIC LUPER is an author. When he is not doing this important work, he is also a spine doctor. He has written books for kids of all ages, including a bunch for Cartoon Network. Eric lives in Albany, New York with his wife, two kids, and two betta fish named Ginger and Houdini.

WHERE EVERY PUPPY FINDS A HOME

Puppy Powers

Get your paws on the
Puppy Powers series!

Puppy Powers
A Wishbone
Come True
KRISTIN EARHART
SCHOLASTIC

Puppy Powers
Wag,
You're It!
KRISTIN EARHART
SCHOLASTIC

Puppy Powers
Take a
Bow-Wow
KRISTIN EARHART
SCHOLASTIC

Puppy Powers
Hide and
Go Fetch
KRISTIN EARHART
SCHOLASTIC

There's something special about the animals at
Power's Pets . . . something downright magical!